# Hotwife Hotel Cheating Exposed - A Wife Watching Hot Wife Romance Novel

Karly Violet

Published by Karly Violet, 2021.

This is a work of fiction. Similarities to real people, places, or events are entirely coincidental.

HOTWIFE HOTEL CHEATING EXPOSED - A WIFE WATCHING HOT WIFE ROMANCE NOVEL

**First edition. November 8, 2021.**



ISBN: 979-8201988739

Written by Karly Violet.

# Hotel Hotwife Cheating Exposed

# A Wife Watching Hot Wife Romance Novel



Individuals on the cover are models and are used for illustrative purposes only.

Author's note: All character in this story are 18 years of age and older. This is a work of fiction, any resemblance to real live name or events are purely coincidental.

Be aware: This story is written for, and should only be enjoyed by, ADULTS. It includes explicit descriptions of intense sexual activity between consenting adults.

**Note that this work of fiction resembles a fantasy world, all events taking place are a result of a role play amongst all parties and all parties are fully consenting adults.**

**This ebook should be purchased/borrowed by and read by adults only.**

# Chapter One: Too Busy to Care

I can never seem to get away from work. As the regional manager for a large department store chain, I have a lot to do to keep our region's stores as profitable as possible. Unfortunately, that means that when there are weak links in the chain that I have to eventually deal with them. One way or the other.

"It's that television star, Wyatt Felton," someone says in the breakroom as I sit at my table in the corner. One of the worst things the company bosses could have done is to put a television in here. Sure, people like to watch the news sometimes while on their lunch breaks, but I prefer to sit in peace and quiet to let my mind wander as I need it to so that I can somewhat organize my thoughts. In this case, I need to decide what the hell to do about the two store managers whose sales numbers are lackluster at best.

"He's got a wife, though, right?" someone else in the breakroom says. "And he's out with another woman?"

"Who gives a shit?" I say under my breath as I go back to looking over the sales stats from both underperforming stores. Maybe there's a logical reason for both locations to have fallen so much in the last quarter? I really should go ask the store managers personally.

"They have video," someone else in the room says as he laughs. "That guy's wife is going to screw him over in divorce court. You don't do something like that in front of the cameras. Especially not if you're so well known."

"Fucking stupid," I mutter about the newscast. My mind goes back to the conversation I had yesterday with Aaron Michaelson, one of the store managers and a friend of mine from college.

"We've had an off few months," he told me over the phone. "We're coming back, though. We have a couple of huge sales coming down the pike and I think this will really bring in the customers, Owen."

"We can't wait forever," I informed him during that phone call. "Ray and the other vice presidents are calling for heads to roll wherever profits aren't being made. If you can't show that things are turning around, I don't know where this goes, man."

"Come on, Owen. You know me. I'm good at this. I'll get the ship back on course."

"You got a store that already was on course for nearly double last year's earnings, Aaron. They can see that things dropped when you took control of the place. This sort of thing might not be so bad at a mom and pop establishment, but we're talking about a national retailer. The newspapers will have a field day with this when the numbers come back out and our investors will be royally pissed." I normally don't worry about investors myself. That's the job of the higher-ups. However, I feel that my old friend needs to have a good understanding of what's going to happen if things don't get better very quickly.

"I'll get it back. Give me six more months. I promise." That's pretty much where we left off with yesterday's phone call. I told him there would be a thirty-day review soon and there had to be something that I could take back to Ray and the other bosses. If not, Aaron's job was in play. He might need to consider where else he could go.

"Shameless slut," one of the women in the breakroom says as she watches the television. "Homewrecking bitch."

"He's the one doing it too," another employee responds. "Is he a shameless slut and a homewrecker, too?"

"That's different. The woman obviously seduced him."

"Linda, is that the way you women always do things? You seduce the men around you?" I have become tired of this conversation, so I get up and make my way back to my office. Once inside, I close the door and go straight to my desk.

"Dammit, Aaron," I say as I see a text message appear on the screen of my phone.

"Look, I know the earnings report is bad, but just hear me out. I'm trying." The message actually sounds like someone begging for his job. It's a far cry from the rugby player I once knew in college. Why does Aaron plead with me like this? He knows I don't like texting in the first place.

"Time's limited," I tell him. "We spoke yesterday about this. Thirty days."

"Yeah, I know," he texts back to me. "But you have some pull with Ray. He'll listen to you, buddy. Give me a chance. I'll make it all back and then some."

I shake my head as I put my cell phone down. Aaron is not the only manager who will likely lose his position. Charlie Blanton is also sitting in a store that seems unable to do any better than it has for the last few quarters. He's been the manager there for three years and we have seen just a few bright spots in the earnings there. However, they tend to be short lived and very scant. The general trend has been down, and so Charlie will probably be losing his job as well. I hate the idea of this for both men, but there's really not much that I can do about their situations.

"Unless I go to each store and run them myself for a while," I posit as I sit down in my chair. It wouldn't be the first time I've done such a thing. Sometimes store managers need to see an example of how to run their operations. I have helped a few stores become leading earners simply by coming in and taking over for a week or so. The only problem with that is that I'm not paid to be a store manager. Ray has pointed that out on more than one occasion. Besides, my old friend Aaron has already discounted this possibility with me. He doesn't need to be *'babysat.'*

My cell phone rings. It's my wife, so I answer the call. "Hey, sexy lady."

"Hey yourself," she says with a giggle. "I thought I would check in with you from the windy city of Chicago."

"Lots of wind there?"

"I can't keep my hair in place," Cassie replies with a laugh. We have been married for five years and I still love to hear her voice over the phone. She knows just how to lighten my day when things aren't what they should be.

"How's the pharma conference? Learning anything new?"

She sighs. "Not really. Things are slow here and the company reps are beating around the bush about some new products they want to present to us. You know, if they could just shoot straight with us, we could sell their new medications to the doctors a little easier." Cassie has been a pharmaceutical representative since before I met her. Her college degree is in biochemistry, which makes her a great choice for showcasing the newest medicines when approaching doctors. She's damned good at her job, which is why her company sends her to these conferences quite often.

"I miss you," I tell her as I smile to myself. "Fucking your pillow is getting boring."

Cassie laughs. "My pillow had better be clean when I get back, Owen. I swear, if it's crusty from your..." She stops there and begins to laugh again. This causes me to laugh as well. Hearing her over the phone this morning has just about made up for the concerns that I have at work.

"Your pillow is fine. When do you think you'll be back?" I ask.

"Probably by Friday afternoon. At least, that's what things look like right now. I'll let you know if there's a need to stay a day or two longer."

"Alright. I look forward to seeing you soon, though."

"Me too, sweetie. Have a good day at work. I love you."

"I love you too." I hear my wife hang up on the other end of the call and I slowly put my own cell phone down on my desktop. Though I miss Cassie and would love to talk to her all day, I have a job to do. I need to decide how to handle the two managers whose stores are tanking. It's not an easy decision to make, but one that is important nonetheless.

"Fucking hell, Aaron. Why can't you do your job and get those numbers up?" I look at the report for the sixth time this morning and try to think of how I can avoid letting him go. It doesn't help that I've gotten another three text messages from him over the last minute.

"You know I'm a good manager," he tells me in one message. "Come on, talk to me, Owen," he says in the second one. The third message sounds as if he's coming a little unhinged. "You can at least fucking fire me to my face, dammit! Talk to me! Reply, Owen!" An angry emoji follows the final message. I shake my head. Maybe I was wrong to hire an old college friend for a position like store manager. Maybe I should have told him that there were no jobs available for him at my company when he asked last year. Unfortunately, what's done is done and now I have to deal with those consequences. Either I'll have to do my job here or Ray will see me as not being a good fit in my own position. I can't have that. No, if things don't change rapidly in Aaron's store, he'll have to be let go. There will be no other option for me.

# Chapter Two: Things Couldn't Be Clearer

Being home without Cassie just doesn't feel like home. Even so, I'm tired after a long day at work and I need some rest in front of the television while I eat my Chinese take-out. After making myself comfortable by kicking off my shoes, I sit back in my recliner and open the top of the food container.

"And Wendy, what news do we have about a certain celebrity this evening?" a news anchor on the television asks a young woman in a video shot in front of a large hotel.

"Well, Danny, I'm here in Chicago where Wyatt Felton has been staying for the last few days. As many already know, he's set to appear in his first major movie role next year, and filming is just wrapping up on location here. Although you might expect that this would be the big news about Mr. Felton, it is not." A video begins to play and I shake my head.

"Another fucking actor. Who the hell cares?" I reach for the television remote. As I begin to change the channel, I see several people clambering with cameras inside the Embassy Suites Hotel in Chicago. It's where Cassie is staying, so I figure that maybe I will watch and have something to talk with her about later.

"Wyatt, who is she?" The camera pans in and I can see the actor, a huge grin on his face, walking beside a young woman who's wearing large sunglasses and a hat. I sit forward as I look closely at her.

"What is that?" I squint my eyes and finally I'm able to see a dove tattoo on the inside of her arm, just above her wrist. It looks a lot like the one my wife Cassie has on her arm as well. At first, I dismiss this as just a coincidence. But then I notice the style of the sunglasses and the hat. Both of them are exactly the sort that I gave Cassie for her birthday last year. Even the tee shirt looks familiar to me.

"Bullshit," I chuckle as the location reporter, Wendy, comes back into the shot.

"Wyatt Felton has so far refused to discuss with paparazzi or the media who this unnamed woman is. However, his wife Charlise Felton has put out a press statement which announces that she has filed for divorce from her husband citing irreconcilable differences. Back to you, Danny."

"Amazing," the first anchor says inside the news studio. He looks at his partner and asks, "Why would someone cheat on his wife like that when his wife happens to be an international runway model?"

"One can never tell why some people do what they do in their marriages," the woman beside him says. "All we can do is keep an eye on this story as it develops." She looks into the camera and continues, "In other news..." I turn off the television with the remote as I shake my head. After putting my box of fried rice down, I get up from my chair and pace the floor for a moment.

"There's just no fucking way," I say over and over again as if I'm trying to convince someone. "Cassie would never do that sort of thing to me. Never. She loves me too much." I look over at my cell phone and get an idea. After picking it up, I sit back down in my recliner and open up the web browser. I type in the actor's name and then scroll through the search results. It doesn't take long to find all sorts of photographs and videos online of the two people together.

There is a string of pictures of them inside a very nice restaurant. The woman looks a lot like Cassie, but I still can't be sure from the angle at which the photograph has been shot. Then there's a video or two that comes up on the same website. I watch those for a couple of minutes. There's not much to go on from these either. As I become convinced that I'm mistaken in who I think the woman is, I find one last video that was taken near a swimming pool at the hotel. Wyatt Felton is passionately kissing a topless woman. When they pull back from each other, I can see her face clearly.

*"Fuck!"* I toss my phone to the sofa and get up from my chair. *"FUCK!!!"* I grit my teeth and swing my fist through the air as I realize Cassie is screwing the actor behind my back. "Honestly? We're hardly even five years into our marriage and you're fucking some asshole from

*Hollywood?!"* I seethe as I look around the room and try to get my thoughts in order. *"Motherfucker."*

I stop for a moment and try to catch my breath as I think about my marriage to Cassie. What should I do? Should I call her and confront her now? Or do I get a divorce attorney and do what the guy's wife is apparently doing? It's not the sort of thing that I would have considered just this morning as I got ready for work. As far as I was concerned, I was still in a strong and loving marriage in which Cassie and I despised being apart. Apparently she's having sex with someone while away from me, though.

My cock gets hard and I'm shocked at the reaction. "Why the hell?" I shake my head and pick up my phone. "What the fuck are you doing?" I type into a text message box. I almost send it, but then I erase the message. Is this the best way to handle what's going on with her in Chicago? Or would it be better to confront her physically? For a moment I consider buying the next airplane ticket to the windy city, but I decide against such action. No, I need time to think. I don't need to act too rashly toward Cassie or the situation that she has placed us in.

My heart thumping inside my chest hard, I sit back down and pick the fried rice container back up. After taking a bite, I shake my head and mutter," That's not fair, Cassie. Not fair at all. I'm faithful to you and you go and fuck some actor. A fucking *actor!"* I put the container aside again and just sit back in my chair. Crossing my arms, I consider all that's on my proverbial plate right now.

"I have a friend from college screwing up and about to lose his damned job," I say to myself. "Earnings reports from my particular region are down," I add. "And now my fucking wife is having an affair while millions of people watch. It's only a matter of time before everyone we know finds out about this. I'm left here as the damned cuckold." My cock again swells a little as I think about Cassie's legs over the other man's shoulders, her feet swinging wildly as he pumps hard into her pussy with his large dick. Why am I hard? What about this turns me on so much?

My cell phone buzzes. I look down at it and I'm shocked by who it is. "Are you home?" Cassie asks me in a text message.

I pick up the phone and think about just ignoring her. However, that might only cause worry. "And we wouldn't want to do that, would we?" I say to myself sarcastically. "I'm home," I answer plainly in a return text message.

"Good! How was your day?" What the fuck does she mean by that? I've just found out that she likes to hang out with and screw actors.

"Okay," I reply.

"Good!" She adds a smiling emoji to this particular text message. "I'm also doing very well. It's been a busy afternoon."

"I'll bet." I don't send this as a text message, but say it under my breath. "You normally are very busy at these things," I answer her. "I hope you're getting plenty of rest, though." Why don't I just come out and tell her that I know? For pete's sake, it's already all over the news. Even my coworkers and friends are going to recognize that this actor's new fuckmate is my wife!

"Have you been missing me?" Cassie sends several lip and heart emojis after the question. "I've been missing you, baby."

"Dammit." I want to tell my wife to fuck off and then block her number. However, she's still my wife. Even though she's letting another man poke her, we are still tied to each other by our vows and I'll be fucked with a dry cucumber in the ass if I'm going to be the one who ends things.

"Owen?" She is expecting me to answer. I guess I'll have to.

"I'm here. I've missed you a lot." I choke back a few choice words as I write the text message to her. "Please come home soon." I avoid the emoji board. I just can't bring myself to send anything sweet to Cassie at this moment. Not after seeing her on the television with Wyatt Felton.

"I can't wait to see you on Friday when I get back," she says with more emojis. "We'll have dinner then, okay?"

"Yeah, okay," I reply. What will I say to my wife when she gets back? What I've seen today has upended my life and likely changed my marriage to the woman that I thought would be mine and only mine for the rest of my life. Things are going to be so difficult for me to figure out between now and then. Even so, I don't want to confront her by text message.

"I love you, Owen. I'll see you when I get back."

"Yeah, I'll see you then." This is the last of our conversation before I sit back down on the recliner and just stare at the Chinese takeout cartons nearby. "Dammit, Cassandra Lynn," I moan as I lean back in my seat. "You have fucking ended us, haven't you? This movie star is better than me, huh? He's got money and a great body. I don't have the best of either one, I suppose." I've thought about working out more at the gym, but work has kept me from making that commitment to improving my physique.

Looking down at my phone, I again decide to do some internet sleuthing. I soon happen upon even more photographs and videos being posted by amateur and professional paparazzi alike. Much of this will likely make its way into the national newspapers and news programs on television by tomorrow. Though I would like to keep this marital issue just between Cassie and I, the whole world will soon know. The press might even come to me for a statement.

"Fucking journalists. Fucking actors. They're all fucking dicks," I gripe as I shake my head. Money is what drives everything on television and in the papers. I know that as well as anyone else does. Still, it doesn't help that they will use my wife to promote their advertisers. The stink of Hollywood has come to my door and I don't like it one bit.

My phone rings. It's my brother Theo, so I take the call. "Hey, bro! How's it hanging?"

I smile a little before answering, "To the left and further down than yours."

My brother chuckles. “Only because you’re shorter than me.” I allow a laugh as for a split second Cassie and her lover leave my mind. Unfortunately, she comes right back to the top of my thoughts almost immediately.

“What’s up?” I ask.

“Nothing much. I’m just checking to see if you and Cassie will be joining the family at the reunion next month. It’s at the large pavilion at the park in Lake City.”

I grimace. “I’m not sure we’ll make it then, Theo.”

“Oh? You have both been showing up each year, Owen. What’s up?”

I don’t want to share what’s going on with Cassie and the actor yet. He will know soon enough and I want to enjoy some relative peace before it gets out that my wife is a slut.

“We’re both probably going to be working. You know how Cassie can be with her pharmaceutical stuff. I think she has a conference to go to that weekend.”

“Oh, man, that sucks,” he replies. “You can still come, though, right?”

Swallowing hard, I reply, “I’ll try to be there. It just depends on a lot of things. The shit is hitting the fan in my region because I have a couple of terrible managers at stores that are not performing well. I’m probably going to have to fire them both.”

“Hey, drop a piano on those goons and get things right!” Theo has a way with words sometimes. He isn’t aware that one of those so-called goons is a good friend of mine from college.

“I’ll deal with them soon. So, you can put me down as a *maybe* for the reunion date. I don’t think Cassie will make it, though.”

“Damn, bro. Everything okay between the two of you?” My younger brother has always had a sixth sense about things like relationships. It’s honestly a little creepy.

“Don’t worry, Theo. As of right now, we’re still together.” I chuckle as I try to cover my concern about my marriage to Cassie. I love her and I still want her as my wife, but that will be completely up to her.

Unfortunately, I don't have a mansion or a home on the Mediterranean Sea to tempt her to stay with me.

"That's good. I really like seeing you both together. You two were made for each other." Theo clears his throat and says, "I'll let you go, man. Just getting numbers for Mom. You know how she can be."

"I know. It's good to talk to you."

"You too. Love you, bro."

"I love you too." We hang up and I lay my cell phone down on the recliner arm. I don't sit for long before getting up and going to the bathroom. I need a shower. A cold shower. Tomorrow will likely be full of new revelations on the news programs, which means Cassie's identity won't be hidden for long. When it comes to a curious press, they can find out practically anything. There's just nowhere she can hide.

# Chapter Three: Personal Dilemma

"Good morning, Owen. Come on in!" The middle-aged company vice president, Ray Burkes, invites me into his office. "Have a seat." I make my way toward his desk, my heart racing inside my chest. I have known Ray since beginning my job at the corporate offices here and he's been nothing but a great guy to me. Funny and modest, the man is a pleasure to work for. However, he's called me in here today to talk about the regional sales report.

"I know you've seen the numbers," I tell him as he makes himself comfortable behind his desk. "I'm looking at what needs to be done about the two stores that are losing profit."

"They're hemorrhaging, Owen," Ray replies as he puts on his reading glasses and looks at the laptop screen in front of him. "It's been months of declining sales and nothing has changed. You need to fix this problem soon." His dark blue eyes look up at me as he removes his glasses. Though a kind man, he can be straight to the point when he needs to be.

"Yeah, I know. I'll have to do whatever's necessary to shore up sales and get the trajectory to reverse."

He sighs. "Look, I know Aaron is a friend of yours, but he can't cut it, Owen. We have high expectations of our managers, and I'm afraid that he's not exactly towing the line for the company."

"It's a difficult location," I offer. "When he took the job, sales were already weakening. I think that with the right help he can be a great manager."

Ray nods his head. "Perhaps you're right. I'm just not sure that he's a good fit for our company, though." The vice president of the company shakes his head. "I'll leave this in your hands, though. I know you are very capable in what you do and I don't want to step on your toes. Still, I think you need to carefully consider what his presence is saying to other managers at other stores in your region. I'm sure some of them are curious as to how Aaron still has a job."

"I know. I'm going to talk to him, Ray. I promise."

"I know you will. You always do the right thing." He sits back and looks at me for a moment before asking, "Do you mind if we discuss what could be a sensitive private matter?"

"Sure. What is it?"

Ray sighs. "I've seen the news, Owen. A lot of other folks here have seen it as well. People are noticing who she is."

My heart pounds hard. "Are you talking about the Wyatt Felton thing?"

"Yes I am. They identified the woman this morning on the news. Did you see that?" I feel utterly embarrassed as I look away from my boss's gaze. Dammit, now Cassie's affair has come to haunt me even at work. No part of this can be private any longer.

"I didn't see it, but I found out last night," I tell him. "I'm sorry about how this might look for the company."

Ray chuckles. "Fuck the company, Owen. This is about you and your marriage. Is it over between the two of you?"

"I don't know," I answer honestly. "I haven't spoken to her about it yet."

"You didn't call her when you found out? She didn't call you?" I shake my head. "Holy shit, Owen. You have to do or say something. You can't just ignore this as it goes on in the press."

"Yes, sir, I know. It's just that I don't know what to say or do just yet. When I texted with Cassie last night, she acted like nothing was going on. I did too. I guess I'm afraid to face whatever will happen to us when we finally talk about what's going on." I fight back a few tears as I stoically look at my boss. Here I am, supposedly a strong regional manager, almost crying in Ray Burke's office. No, I won't allow myself to do that. I won't.

"My ex-wife pulled something similar with me a few years ago," he begins to tell me as he leans back in his chair. "She decided that she would have an affair behind my back, but with someone I knew really well."

"I'm sorry to hear that."

"My brother," he offers as he shakes his head and laughs. "My own fucking brother. Talk about a shot in the back. She was having sex with him in my home while our kids were asleep in their bedrooms. Apparently he would come over when I left for work." His eyes turn back to me. "It was a mistake moving into the same cul de sac as my brother and his wife, but we did. Anyway, he started making moves on my wife and one day she just gave in to him. My entire family knew about it before I did. Hell, she even had divorce papers served on me while we were having a cookout with the kids in the backyard."

"She left you for your brother?"

"Not really, no. She had been with him, but he reconciled with his wife and she then decided she was done with me. So, she embarrassed me right in front of my own children while I served her a hamburger."

"Shit, Ray. I didn't know." I knew the vice president of regional operations was divorced. However, the entire thing happened before I came to work for the company. I've simply never asked him about any of the juicy details and up until now he hasn't offered any. After hearing the story, I don't feel quite as terrible about my own situation with Cassie.

"You have to confront her and figure out what to do, Owen. Don't let her dictate the terms, either. If this is really the end of your marriage, it needs to be mutually acceptable." He pauses. "I don't recall the two of you having children. Is that correct?"

"No kids," I tell him quickly. "We've just been too busy for anything like that."

"Maybe it's for the best." Ray smiles at me. "I don't mean to bring you down, but I thought it might help you to know my story. Things will be tough, but I have every confidence that you can weather this storm, Owen. I know you can." He smiles at me before standing up from his seat and walking over to the window behind his desk.

"Thanks for the advice." I begin to get up, but he turns to look at me.

"The two stores, Owen. You need to get them under control, but I can see where maybe you need some time to mull things over. Take the next couple of weeks off and take care of your personal affairs. Maybe you can fix things with your wife. However, I don't know that she has left you many options with the way that she's made this so public."

"I don't have to take off from work, Ray. I'm fine."

"Just take it, Owen. It won't count against you. You're a fine regional manager and you need to deal with whatever is happening with your wife and that celebrity." Turning to look at me, Ray adds, "I would break his fucking nose if I were you. Not that I'm saying that you should." He allows a devilish grin as he goes back to his desk. "Take a couple of weeks and then come back. I'll want to know what you will be doing about the two managers of those stores when you return. Try to relax a little, too."

"Um, I will." I get up from my chair and make my way to the office door. After opening it, I step out to see Ray's personal secretary working on something at her desk. She looks up at me and smiles for a moment. Then a look of half-hearted pity begins to creep across her face. She knows. They probably all know. All I can do for now is nod my head and go to the elevator for the ride down to my floor.

"Dammit. It's already begun," I say to myself as I ride the elevator down. Though yesterday no one in the company recognized my wife on the news, they now are. She's been identified by the journalists and it won't take long for those same journalists to find me as well.

The elevator door opens and I walk out. Two of my coworkers nearby look over at me for a moment, but then look away. They begin to talk to each other about something as they lean toward each other over a desk. Even my own floor isn't a safe place for me anymore. Everyone knows that my wife Cassie is fucking Wyatt Felton. Though that might be a dream come true for a lot of women here, it disgusts me in a terrible way. If I could, I would take Ray's advice and break the man's nose. The only problem is that I wouldn't be able to get close enough to him to do it. He likely has plenty of bodyguards surrounding him.

"I'm so sorry," Janey Powell says from her desk just outside my office. Janey has worked as my receptionist for the last few months. "If there's anything that I can do, just let me know."

"I'm fine," I tell her before walking into my office and closing the door behind me. Settling down behind my desk, I pull out my cell phone and check to see if I've missed any text messages from Cassie. I might not have been willing last night to talk about what has been happening behind my back, but now I am. If she messages me or calls, our conversation will be less than cordial.

"All over the fucking news," I mutter as I look at a popular news site on my phone. "Everyone knows. They'll bug me about it soon. Damn you, Cassie." My face is hot as it turns deep red. "Even our family will know. Theo." Shaking my head, I think about calling him. I don't, though. My brother will have nothing but jokes to throw my way and I'm just not in the mood for that right now. No, I'll wait until they hear about this and contact me. I don't want to be the one to tell my mother either.

My cell phone buzzes with a text message. It's from Cassie and it simply offers a heart emoji and then another with a face full of tears. What she means by this, I don't know. I begin to compose my reply, but then I think better of it. My wife probably wants to talk now instead of face me in person. That's not how I do things in my line of work or in my personal life. No, I won't entertain a text message reply to her. She'll have to talk to me in person when she returns from her fucking trip.

"After being your husband for five years, you go and find another man. How very nice, Cassie. How very nice indeed." I close my laptop and get up from my seat. Going to the door, I turn off the lights and let Janey know that I will be taking off the next couple of weeks. She nods her understanding and I make my way to the elevator. My wife is due to be home in a couple of days. I'll wait to see her to answer her message in person.

# Chapter Four: More Evidence

Home isn't exactly the best place to be when having something like a wife's infidelity hanging over a guy's head. At least, that's what I'm finding out as I fill my time with television and reading the news online. The news sucks. If it's not about Cassie and that celebrity fuck, it's about someting almost just as pointless.

"Dammit." I cringe as I come across another news article concerning Wyatt Felton and my wife.

*"Mr. Felton's wife has decided to ask for half of his earnings for the last three years of their marriage. Mrs. Felton claims that it's what's owed to her for her devotion to her celebrity estranged husband. We'll see if a judge agrees when she goes to court next month."*

"I don't give a shit," I grumble as I finish reading the short article on Yahoo News. "He deserves to have everything stripped away from him after going after some other man's wife."

I wonder what Cassie is thinking about all this right now? She hasn't said anything to me about it yet, but surely she's been seeing the photographs and the news reports. After all, she's a pharmaceutical representative with a degree in biochemistry. Cassie is far from a moron and typically keeps up with current events.

My phone rings. I answer it and find that my boss is on the other end of the line. "Just checking in," he says to me. "How are you doing, Owen? I was told that you left the office yesterday pretty upset."

I sigh. "I don't know, Ray. I haven't heard from my wife yet."

"You haven't called her?" Ray's voice gives me the sense that he's judging me a little for not contacting Cassie before now. However, I know that he understands how difficult this is after going through some shit with his own ex-wife.

"No, not yet. I just can't get the guts up to do it," I reply. "What she's done is beyond belief. People will be talking about it for a very long time."

"Maybe," he replies. "Still, she's your wife and you need to get some answers from her. It's painful, I know, but you can't let things slide. You need to call her."

"I'll think about it," I promise. "In the meanwhile, I spoke to Aaron. He's working on a plan to improve his store, Ray. Please give him a chance."

The regional vice president sighs. "You're his supervisor, Owen. It's up to you in the short term as to what happens, but if he can't fix things there he'll have to go." He pauses and then adds, "You shouldn't be concerned about work while you're off, though. Don't worry, I'm not going to fire anyone without consulting with you first."

I smile as I think about Ray and how hard he's worked for the company over the time that I've known him. There are few other people in our business who are willing to let their managers do their job without intervening. I've seen plenty of other bosses at the corporate level who are more than happy to micromanage things. It usually puts middle management in a terrible light with those who work for them. I'm glad Ray is my immediate supervisor.

"I'll try to call Cassie later. Maybe. If I have a stiff drink or two first."

"You do that. Call me when you know something, Owen. I'm here for you." Ray hangs up and I put my cell phone down on the arm of the recliner. The television is on a local channel and thankfully there's currently no discussion about Wyatt Felton and his slutty lover.

"What to do?" I ask myself as I look at my phone. Against my better judgement, I search online for Wyatt Felton and come up with even more photos and videos of the two of them together. There are some pictures that show them at an ice cream bar together and some others that involve them being at least partially nude. Suddenly, I happen upon a gossip website that claims to have video.

*"The mainstream news will never run this video in its entirety! For less than ten bucks, get a monthly subscription to our site to see Wyatt Felton*

*with his new girlfriend while in bed."* My lips turn down as I think about the website's claim to have a sex video of the two of them together.

"There's no way someone could have gotten in there and filmed them," I say to myself as I look at the sign-up form for the website. Do I give them money just to see if the video is real? Or maybe this is just an attempt by the owners to profit off the latest Hollywood scandal. Either way, I need to know. So, I put in my information, as well as a credit card number, and become a subscriber to the site. Then I make my way to the video. It's already been watched more than fifty thousand times. The owners are making a killing in subscription fees with my wife's indiscretions.

I click play and watch as the two people in bed roll around with each other. They have no clothes on and I can quickly make out that my wife is one of them. Cassie goes down on the celebrity and draws his pecker into her mouth, sucking on him hard as she tussles his balls with one of her hands. I get hard as I see her pleasuring him.

"Fuck, Cass," I say quietly as I move my cock around to give it more room inside my shorts. Why this makes me so horny doesn't make any sense. As I continue to watch, Wyatt soon flips her over and pushes her legs back. It takes him no time to slide his johnson into my wife's moist pussy. He fucks her hard, his balls slapping her asshole, sounding as if someone is in the room clapping for them. I don't think I've thrust so hard before as he moves Cassie's petite body across the bed with each thrust.

"Oh, Wyatt," she moans as she plays with her nipples. "Fuck me hard, Wyatt. Make me come."

"I'm coming, baby!" His back arches as Wyatt begins to release into her tight muff. *"Gahhh...ohhh...ohhh..."* He holds on hard to Cassie's hips as he empties his ball juice into her.

*"Baby! OH, BABY!!!"* My wife orgasms as he pushes his dick as far as he can into her pussy. I pre-come a little as I move my junk around inside

my pants again. *"Uh...uhhhh..."* They roll up together on the bed and the video suddenly shuts off.

"That's it?" I say as I look at the timer at the bottom of the video. "Two minutes and thirteen seconds? That's all they have?" I don't know if it's my horniness or the fact that I feel like I've been cheated of whatever else was said or done before the actual intercourse happened. I know Cassie. She likes to play around for at least an hour or so before she gets off.

"Damn video." I close the website and put my phone back down. I'm confused about why I'm so horny over the video and pictures I have seen. Why does it turn me on when I see my wife in these situations with the other man? Is there something wrong with me?" I pick my phone back up and search for the answer to this very question. As I look online, I find websites and forums dedicated to husbands who like that their wives are unfaithful to them. Some of them even encourage them to go find other men.

"That's not a good thing," I say as I read some of the comments in a forum. One man has written that his wife has been having an affair behind his back for the last year. He just found out that it is his neighbor and so now he peeps on them. He also has installed cameras in his own home to catch her with the other guy while he's away on work trips.

Another website is a blog where a husband and wife detail their experiences with her unfaithfulness. She goes and has sex with other men and only tells her husband about it when she comes home. This gets him off. They have sex while talking about some of her lovers.

"Still getting hard," I say as I shake my head. "Why are you like this, Owen? That guy is a douche bag and you know it. He's screwing your wife and making a mockery out of your marriage."

There's not a lot that I can do to stop the raging boner in my shorts unless I do something about it. So, I pull my shorts leg to the side and fish my cock out with my hand. Stroking it, I pre-come a bit more as I pull up the same video on my phone again and watch it.

"Fuck, honey," I moan as I watch my wife shafted over and over by her celebrity lover. "He's going to come inside you," I say as I pull hard on my cock. "Dammit, he's going to jizz inside you, Cassie. He's going to leave his spunk inside your tight pussy." I breathe hard as I feel my balls tighten. "You fucking whore. Oh, you fucking whore...*ahhhh!!!*" A long spurt of white sauce ejects from the tip of my manhood as I squeeze it hard. *"Uhhh...uhhh...uhhh..."* I keep stroking myself as I watch the two naked people in bed together. This time around, I can see some of Wyatt's spunk slowly oozing from my wife's pussy after he pulls out of her. *"Fuck..."*

I finish my orgasm and shove my wet cock back into my shorts. I've made a mess on myself, the chair, and the floor. "Bullshit," I growl as I get up to find something to wipe off with. I go to the kitchen to find a small hand towel so that I can clean the wet sauce from my shorts and legs.

"You fucking whore," I say of my wife as I think about Wyatt Felton's DNA draining out of her. "Fifty thousand people have seen you do that," I add as if she's in the room with me. Of course, Cassie isn't anywhere nearby. She's all the way in Chicago, Illinois and apparently not all that concerned with what I might think about what she's been up to. I'm not sure whether I'm more offended with the way she's cheating on me or the fact that she's flaunting it in public. Though I could spend more time obsessing over these questions, I need a shower. It might help to wash away some of the thoughts I've had today.

# Chapter Five: An Intense Conversation

As I settle back into my bed, the cell phone on my nightstand rings. It's Cassie, and at first I consider not answering it at all. However, I know that I can't avoid her forever. She's coming home soon, after all.

"Hello?" I say as I answer the call.

"Hey, babe. I didn't catch you in bed already, did I?"

I take a quick breath. "No. I was just getting ready to go to bed."

"Good. So, how's your week going?" I can't believe that Cassie would ask me this. How's my week going? Gee, I don't know. My wife is on the fucking evening news with her lover and my boss at work knows about it. Along with all my coworkers. And every fucking person in the state as well as a large number from here to Hollywood, California. My week is going great. Fuck you.

"I'm okay," I lie as resentment festers deep inside me. "I hope you're getting your work done there in Austin." I know better. The only job she's working is the one that involves her mouth on Wyatt Felton's erect cock.

"I'll be home Friday. Everything has gone off without a hitch." She pauses for a moment and I wonder whether she might finally come clean with me about what she's up to. "We should go back to that Italian restaurant that we visited a couple of months ago. Maybe this weekend. What's the name of it again?"

I know the place very well. We were both very pleased with the offerings on the menu. *"Kitchen Italiano,"* I reply.

"Yeah, that's the one," she answers with a slight giggle. "I can't wait to see you, Owen. It's been far too long."

"Has it?" I let this slip without much thought as my mind decides whether I should just hang up on my wife.

"What do you mean?" she asks.

"Nothing," I reply. "Just forget about it." There is another moment or two of strained silence over the phone.

"Are you alright?"

"Seriously? You're asking me that, Cass? Am I alright? I don't know, honey. Am I?"

She doesn't answer for a few seconds, but then responds, "What's wrong, Owen?"

I grit my teeth as I try to keep from flying into a rage. My wife is fucking another man. And not just any other man, but a fucking celebrity. The embarrassment factor just keeps rising for me as I've faced others at work and elsewhere who already know about the lurid details. I can only imagine that there's going to be questions from the press directed toward me very soon.

"Are you really this clueless, Cassie? Don't you watch the damned news? Haven't you seen the fucking cameras when you and loverboy have been out and about? Dammit. You're making a fucking mockery of our marriage vows!" My voice inflects a little toward the end of my angry retort.

"Owen, I..." Her voice trails off and she becomes silent. My guess is that she now has nothing much to say since I've caught her with her celebrity lover.

"You know, you and that guy make a nice couple. Maybe you should just stay in Chicago and keep his bed warm. I'm sure that he appreciates you so much." My cock gets hard as I think about the two of them together. What the hell is wrong with my body? Why would that thought cause me to be so horny?

"That's not very nice," she replies quietly over the phone.

"Not very nice? Not very *NICE?!"* My anger begins to spill over as I reply. "You have been galavanting around in public with Wyatt Fucking Felton, my love. What the hell are you thinking? There are cameras everywhere and paparazzi have been following this guy for years. Did you have to pick someone like him to screw around with behind my back? *That idiot?"*

"He's not an idiot," Cassie shoots back. "I've never said that I'm sleeping with him, either."

"You don't have to. The news media is already covering it. Did you know that there's video footage of you topless with him? Huh?" I can't believe that she's actually trying to talk her way out of what has been widely reported. "Not to mention the video on one website of the two of you actually...I don't know...*fucking each other.*"

"That's not fair," she answers forcefully. "You can't judge someone that you don't know, Owen. Wyatt is a nice guy." It's obvious that my wife is going to ignore my last statement about the video and the two of them having sex.

"A nice guy who likes to fuck other men's wives. How long has this been going on, Cassie? How fucking long?"

She doesn't answer right away. My guess is that she's trying to find an answer that is the least bit offensive to me as possible. Even so, I'm not going to be happy about it whatever her response ends up being.

"He's a nice guy," Cassie replies as she avoids my question. "This isn't about love, either. We're just good friends."

"Friends with fucking benefits," I complain. "I can't believe that you can sit here on the phone and not even apologize to me for this. Cassie, we have been together for five years. That's not even long enough for the so-called seven-year-itch. Why have you done this?"

"I love you Owen. I'll see you Friday afternoon." She waits for a few seconds, likely hoping that I will respond in kind. However, I do not. Cassie eventually hangs up and I put my phone down on the nightstand as my body shakes.

My phone suddenly rings again. "Fuck me," I growl as I see the unknown number on the screen. "Hello?"

"Owen?"

"Yes."

"Hey, this is Nancy Eaton with Channel Four News. Can we talk about your wife Cassandra and Wyatt Felton?"

"What?" I grimace as I realize that I have finally been found by the journalists looking into the story about the celebrity and his new lover.

"Do you have any comment concerning their public appearances together over the last couple of days in Chicago?"

"I'm not interested," I tell her as my heart races.

"If you could give me just a few minutes of your time, Owen. Have you spoken to your wife? Are you in an open marriage?"

"Dammit, *fuck off!!!*" I hang up the phone and then go to block the number. However, I'm unable to do so as my mind continues to spin with her questions and my fingers aren't working as they should. "A fucking *open marriage?* Where the hell would she get that idea? We're not in a fucking open marriage. Dammit!" I am finally able to block the number and then I turn off my cell phone so that I don't receive any more calls tonight. If one television station has found me, surely more will follow. Journalists can be insidious, after all. They only care about the story and not so much for those who make it up.

"Get a grip on yourself," I say to myself as I get out of bed and walk to the kitchen. After getting a glass from the cabinet, I fill it with water and take a quick drink. I'm sweating and not feeling like going back to bed right now. So, I go to the television and turn it on.

"Wyatt Felton. What a wacky guy, huh? He's going after some other guy's wife." Even a comedy monologue on a late night show involves my wife's dalliances with Felton.

"His wife is pissed," another man says on the show. The audience laughs and cheers.

"Her husband's name is Owen."

"Owen? Like Owen Wilson?"

"Not the same guy, but same first name," the first man replies while the audience laughs. "She must like guys with famous names." They laugh again and it's my cue to change the channel. Now my name is being passed around the airwaves.

"Motherfucking assholes," I spit as I find a nature show to watch. Two antelope are walking quietly beside each other until one of them appears to stop and let the other hump her. Yep. It's mating season for the antelopes and this channel aims to show it off in full color.

"Just like these animals," I mutter as I think about Cassie and the celebrity she has been with this week. "They have been showing themselves off for the cameras. How could she really believe that I didn't know about what she's been up to? Or worse yet, how could she have imagined that I would accept that Wyatt is such a great guy?" I shake my head. Cassie seemed to think that she could convince me that nothing much was going on between them, even though there's video to the contrary. Maybe she really thinks that what they're doing is okay?

"The male antelope is finished doing his part. Now the female will carry her young until full term and birth it out on the prairie. So begins the cycle of life for a young antelope."

"Shit." I turn off the television and get up from my recliner. After going back to the bedroom, I turn my cell phone back on and find several text messages from my wife. I open them up and begin reading.

"You shouldn't be so upset," she says in the first one. The next one tells me, "Wyatt wanted to keep things quiet, but I wanted to go out with him. I don't know why I did it, Owen. Please talk to me."

"Please talk to you? Why? What's there to say after you've let that fucker dip his wick into your honeypot, Cass? Why?" I purse my lips together as I continue to read her text messages to me.

"I love you, Owen. Even if you don't believe me when I say it. I really do." She follows this message with several heart and lip emojis. I snarl in disgust as I get to her final message to me. "Are you really going to be this way? Why don't you answer me back? Talk to me, Owen. Please."

I put my cell phone back on the nightstand. "What do I do?" I ask myself quietly. I do still love my wife. I can't help that. That's probably why I'm so offended at what has happened between her and Wyatt Felton.

We've discussed fantasies with each other in the past. I've always had a thing where I've imagined that someone would come into our home and eat Cassie's pussy. That's never happened, but we've talked about it during sex. She, on the other hand, has always had a little bit of a need for exposure to the public. She sometimes posts risque pictures to Instagram that involve bikini shots and then asks for comments. There are men who occasionally comment, and sometimes I get a little jealous of those guys. But that's been acceptable so far. What I can't understand is why she has taken it so far as to be caught out with a celebrity.

"You could have fucked him quietly," I say into the air. "You didn't have to shove this into my face the way that you have. Now everyone knows, Cassie. Everyone." My cock again is a little more solid than usual. Though I'm a little surprised by the bit of horniness I am feeling for this, I can understand why. My wife is acting out part of her fantasy and that turns me on. It shouldn't, but it does.

My phone rings again. I look at it before hanging up on the person. It's likely another reporter looking for my side of the story. I'm not giving in to their questions, though. As far as I'm concerned, this is a private matter between me and Cassie. Well, as private as it can be at this point. I don't plan to become any more a part of the headlines than I have to.

# Chapter Six: Homecoming

The wait has been a long one. Cassie will be home in a few minutes and I find myself pacing the floor as I work out just what I'm going to say when she gets here. This feeling is so out of place for me, as normally I would be ready to take my dear wife into my arms after being gone for nearly two weeks.

"Calm down," I say to myself as I go to the kitchen and get a glass of water. My hand shakes as I lift the glass to my lips to take a sip. Though refreshing, the water also seems too bland for my current situation. Turning, I reach for a cabinet door where I have a partial bottle of vodka waiting for me. Cassie and I bought the bottle not long after we were first married because we wanted to try it out. Neither of us are really keen on the strong drink, but once in a while we have gotten a glass and had a drink. Right now, it seems that this is exactly the medicine that the doctor has ordered.

After pouring a shot glass full of the clear liquid, I take a drink and realize I've swallowed too quickly. *"Gack!"* I cough a little while closing my eyes and scrunching my face. "Fucking paint thinner," I growl as I put the glass down and turn to take another drink of water. As I walk back into the living room, I hear the doorknob being jostled. My wife has finally returned home.

"Hey," she says with an impish smile as she walks through the door, a small suitcase in her hand. Cassie walks over to me after putting the suitcase down and gives me a tight hug. She then kisses me on the cheek before walking back out to her car to retrieve her other things. In the past, she would have asked me to go and help her with her things, but this time there's no apparent expectation from her that I'll carry anything for her. This change in habit strikes me as strange, but then again I remember our conversation on the phone from the other day. My wife knows that a more difficult conversation between us is waiting to be had.

Cassie soon returns with some more bags and then closes the door behind her. She smiles at me. "Are you glad to see me?" Her smile almost causes my icy disposition to melt, but then I recall what she's been up to with Wyatt Felton for the last two weeks.

"Sure. I'm glad." I strain to say this as I think about the words that I tossed around in my head earlier. There are things that I want to say to my wife that are less than sweet and in some ways very unpleasant.

My wife sighs. "I know we have to talk about what's been going on, but hear me out first, alright?" She focuses her beautiful brown eyes on me. "I met Wyatt a few months ago at another conference in Vegas. I'm a fan of some of his stuff on television, and we struck up a conversation around that. Honestly, that was as far as I expected things between us to go." She pauses, probably to give me the opportunity to say something. I do not, so she continues. "We've been texting a little back and forth since then. Well, when I told him that I would be in Chicago for several days, he decided to fly out and spend some time with me. That's when you started to see the things about us on the news."

I take a breath as I watch Cassie attempt to keep a smile on her face. "Spend some time with you, huh?" Shaking my head, I ask, "How long have you been fucking that loser, Cass?" I feel my face turn red and heat up as I try to keep myself measured and calm. There's no good to come from a man who can't control his own anger.

"He's not a loser, Owen."

"And you didn't answer the question. How long has he been sticking his dick inside you?" This time I'm more crass in the way I ask the question. I want answers. My wife owes me some answers.

Cassie's face turns white as she sits down on the sofa. "We never planned this, you know. This just happened. Things got heated and before we knew it we were being too conspicuous. I told Wyatt that we shouldn't be going outside because of the paparazzi, but he told me it would be okay. All I had to do was wear that stupid hat and sunglasses."

"And a tattoo that is obviously yours," I chime in. "I bought you the fucking sunglasses and hat, Cassie. You actually wore them to try to hide from me? Are you serious?" I sit down in the recliner nearby. "How long?"

My wife fidgets for a moment before replying, "We didn't do anything in Vegas except kiss a little. Things didn't get more involved until we both got to Chicago."

I nod my head as I bite my bottom lip. Finally we're getting somewhere closer to the truth. "And you've been having full sex with him, right?"

"Owen..."

"Say it, Cass." Still calm, I don't know how long I can hold myself together. My own wife is a whore in my mind. She decided to fuck some other man while away from her husband. Not to mention she then broadcast her indiscretions to the whole world.

"Yes. We've been having sex," she admits.

"What kind of sex? Vaginal? Oral? Anal?"

"That's vulgar," she tells me as she looks hard into my eyes. "How could you ask me something like that?"

"How could you do that with another man and then flaunt it in front of the entire fucking world, Cassie? I mean, you couldn't even do it the way that other people do when they cheat. You couldn't screw the guy in private and move on. You had to shove it in my face on national television." Seething with anger, I add, "My entire fucking office knows, Cass. Every damned one of them knows that my wife is screwing that fucking asshole."

"And that's what you're worried about? How other people see you?"

"Not just that, but it makes things worse. I've had television people calling me day and night, Cassie. They want me to comment on why my wife is screwing around with another married man. What am I supposed to tell them?"

"I'm sorry that I've embarrassed you, Owen. Really I am. We were just really into the moment and unfortunately there were people watching our every move."

"Lots of people watching." I lean toward my wife and tell her, "There's even a video online of the two of you having sex. Congratulations. You'll be on PornTV with Wyatt Fucking Felton for years to come." I get up from my seat and walk back to the kitchen. Come to think of it, the strong taste of the vodka is just what I need right now. After pouring myself another shot glass of the strong liquid, I lean back against the countertop and take a quick sip. Cassie walks in and looks at me as well as the bottle of vodka. She reaches into the cabinet and gets herself a shot glass before pouring her own drink.

"You know, we don't have to fight over this. It was a mistake and I'm willing to try to make it up to you, sweetheart."

I chuckle and sarcastically reply, "Oh, you're going to make it up to me, are you? How are you going to do that, my little slut?"

Cassie's eyes narrow at me before she takes a sip of vodka. She puts the glass down and crosses her arms. "I deserve that, I guess." She pauses and then continues. "We had all sorts of sex. Yes, a little vaginal sex. Lots of oral. Some anal. I can't lie to you about that. I'm sorry if that offends you, but things just got a little out of control when Wyatt and I took a room together at the hotel. I tried at first to back away from some of the things we were doing, but he was really convincing." She smiles a little, which causes me to wince.

"Are you in love with him?" I ask while trying to keep myself from insulting Cassie any further.

She quickly shakes her head. "Not at all, Owen. I've never loved another man besides you. You are still the focus of my life. Nothing has changed in the way that I feel about you."

"Yet, you fucked another man and paraded it around on television so that the world would know that my wife is unfaithful to me." I know I sound a bit too sulky as I say this to her, but so what? Cassie has wronged me. I didn't do anything to deserve the attention her little affair has caused me.

"I'm sorry," she tells me. After a moment of reflection, my wife then asks, "Are you going to want a divorce?" Her brown eyes study my face for any sign of an answer. I have considered the answer to this question already, but to be honest, I love Cassie very much. The last thing I could ever want is to end my marriage to her. I simply love her too damned much.

"Did he wear a condom at all?" I ask her as I move past the divorce question. "Or did he just leave it inside you?"

She turns and takes another drink of vodka before putting her empty glass down. Cassie shakes her head as she goes to the dining room table and has a seat. I can see that she's wearing down with our conversation and some part of this feels good to me. I've suffered, after all. Why shouldn't she suffer a little too?

"No condoms," she admits. "But I'm on the pill, so that wasn't a big deal."

My cock gets a little stiff as I think about Wyatt Felton shooting his wad into Cassie's tight little pussy. "How many times did he come inside you?"

Her eyes turn to me. "Again, you're being vulgar, Owen."

"And again, I have the right to ask. You've been putting this all over the news." I shake a little as I realize that I'm turned on by what has happened. Even while reading online news stories and watching videos of the two of them, I have had hardons come up on me. It seems to be a fetish. Some part of me likes that Cassie has been fucked by another man.

"Maybe a dozen times," she replies. "Wyatt is a very sensual man. He likes to do something sexual two or three times each day, and there just wasn't the opportunity to get any condoms."

"And so you gave him blow jobs, right? Did you swallow?"

Cassie looks away. "Yeah, I swallowed."

"And did he taste good?" My cock gets even harder as I watch my wife's facial expressions. Though this must be agonizing for her, I'm enjoying this exchange between us at the moment.

"I don't know about the taste. It wasn't offensive, though."

I quietly finish off my shot glass of vodka before going to the dining room table to stand near her. "Honestly, I don't know what I want to do, Cass. This whole thing has been like a nightmare for me. People calling day and night wanting a scoop on the story, hearing your name on the news...it's been shit for me."

"I know and I'm really very sorry." There are a few tears in Cassie's eyes as she looks over at me. My wife suddenly notices the bulge in the front of my shorts. "Are you hard?"

"No," I say quickly as I take a seat at the table.

"I think you are," she answers me, her wet eyes staring back into mine. "Owen, why are you hard?"

"It's these shorts. The material bunches up sometimes," I reply uneasily as I move around in my seat.

Shaking her head, Cassie stands up from the table. "You're getting off on this, aren't you? The questions you are asking about how many times he came inside me and whether I swallowed are just so that you can jerk off later. That's a little sick, Owen."

"What's sick is to diddle a fucking actor behind my back but in front of the whole damned world, Cassie. Don't try to turn this back onto me when you know that you have been unfaithful to me."

"I see what's going on here," she retorts. "You're mad, sure, but then again you like the thought of it. Owen, be honest; are you getting horny while thinking about me with Wyatt?" Cassie smirks a little as she stares at me. There's no doubt that my wife would like to think that maybe things aren't as bad as I have made them out to be. Maybe I like what she's been doing and I'm not really all that angry with her. I have to admit that I'm a little confused with my own feelings, but I can't let her loop this around in a way that I appear to be alright with her fucking a celebrity.

"You don't know what the fuck you're talking about." I get up from my chair and stomp out of the room. After walking into the bathroom, I close the door and go to stand in front of the mirror. I pull down my shorts to see the raging boner I have and just shake my head. "Why?" I ask myself quietly. This doesn't make sense. Why would I be turned on by what has been happening between my wife and the other man? Haven't I been embarrassed in public and at work because of what they have been up to? If so, how the hell am I so horny?

"I'll be unpacking in the bedroom if you want to talk some more, Owen," Cassie says on the other side of the door. I stand silently and wonder how long this hardon is going to last. The last thing I want to do is go into the bedroom so that my wife can see that I'm still hard. There's only one way to fix this problem. I spit into my hand and begin to rub my pole fast and hard. Only when I've spunked will I be able to keep my manhood flaccid enough to keep from embarrassing myself again.

# Chapter Seven: Awkward Marriage

I haven't seen Cassie all day as I've spent the afternoon on the patio looking out over our backyard. There have been many times in the past when the two of us would enjoy our time out here together, but it seems that could be coming to an end

The sliding glass door opens and my wife steps through it before making her way to a patio chair on the other side of the small table from me. She has a seat and simply smiles. "How has your day been?"

I sigh. "Fine." I don't bother asking the same of her as I continue to gaze out across the well manicured lawn.

"Owen, I need to know the answer to a question I asked you yesterday afternoon. Do you intend to divorce me or not? You owe me an answer."

My heart beats hard as I consider the question. Do I really owe her anything at this point? After all, I haven't been unfaithful to her. As a matter of fact, I think that I've handled things very well when considering the circumstances that I have been faced with.

"I don't think I owe you anything," I tell her. "You are the one who owes me after all the shit you've put me through." I turn and look at her only long enough to see a frown form on her face.

"You were hard last night, Owen. I know you were. I could see it pushing through your shorts. Why were you hard?"

I move around in my seat. "I told you that it was the material in the shorts. It does that sometimes. It wasn't my dick, Cassie."

"Sure it was. I would recognize that outline anywhere." She chuckles before asking, "Are you going to divorce me? I want to know."

"Why?" I focus my eyes on my wife. "What good will it do for you to know whether I want a divorce from you yet? Are you going to get an attorney?"

Cassie shrugs her shoulders. "I don't know, Owen. Am I?" My wife is intent on knowing my answer to the question and I wish that I could give her one. The fact is, I don't want to divorce my wife. However, she did embarrass me in front of my coworkers and friends by showing off her lover on television. How will it play out with them if they find out that all is forgiven and forgotten so easily?

"Look, I haven't made up my mind about anything yet. Divorce isn't something that I take lightly, Cass."

"Neither do I," she replies with a smile. "Which is why I think that you actually like the fact that I've been having intimate relations with Wyatt. That was a hardon in your shorts last night, baby. I've seen it before." Cassie giggles while shaking her head. "You need to just come out and admit that you like the idea of me getting screwed by another man, Owen. There are lots of men just like you." My wife persists in this notion as she seems to take what she's done so lightheartedly. How can she say this to me? Am I not her husband? Yet, there is definitely some truth in her words.

"I don't want to talk about it," I tell her as I turn my attention back to the backyard. "You're not very serious about dealing with this anyway."

"I'm not?" Cassie gets up from her seat and walks over to me. She kneels to the ground and reaches into my shorts leg.

"What are you doing?"

"Proving something." She pulls my cock out and grips it tightly as I get hard. "You still have it bad for me, Owen. Even though I've caused you some pain, you love when I touch you." Cassie spits on the head of my phallus and then uses her hand to rub her oral lubricant around in it.

"Fuck, Cass," I say while feigning mild disgust. "Stop it."

"You stop me," she giggles as she works her small hands up and down my hard pole. "You need to get off, don't you? Last night you probably masturbated in the bathroom, didn't you?" Cassie sees the expression on my face and she lights up. "You did! You jerked off in the bathroom after I noticed your hardon! Wow!" My wife pulls up hard on my cock, causing me to groan deeply.

*"Shit."* I pre-come a little as Cassie works her hands up and down my stalk as well as over the head of it. There's just no hand job like the one my own wife can give me.

"I don't want a divorce and neither do you, Owen. Am I right about that?" She continues to rub my cock.

"No, I don't," I admit. "Fuck."

"And, you like that I had sex with Wyatt, don't you?"

I shake my head as I refuse to answer at first, but she keeps playing with me. "I watched the video of you both together. You were fucking each other," I tell her. "Oh, shit, I loved seeing his balls pound into your asshole so hard, honey."

"*Mmmmm*...you liked that, huh?" Cassie moves one hand to my balls and massages them while continuing to pump me with her other hand. "You would have liked to pound these into my asshole too, right?"

"Dammit," I moan as I move around in my patio chair. "Fuck, I want you so badly, Cassie!"

"Do you, big boy?" My wife releases her grip on me and reaches for the bottom of her tee shirt. She pulls it up over her head to show off her nice, C-cup mammaries. Her large pink nipples are hard in the cool breeze as she pulls down her shorts to reveal her soft, hairless muff. Cassie straddles me and lowers her pussy to my waiting cock, soon swallowing all of it before she bounces slowly up and down.

"Holy fuck," I say while gritting my teeth.

"Feels good, huh?" Cassie says to me as she bends forward and nibbles my ear. She whispers, "This is how I fucked Wyatt the first time, Owen. He really liked that I didn't make him wear a condom. He liked the way the inside of my wet pussy felt on his hard cock." My manhood swells even more as she tells me this and I put my hands on her hips as she grinds into me.

"You fucked him like this?" I say as she sits back and grinds into me.

"Just like this," Cassie replies. Her ass moves back and forth on my lap as she slides the head of my cock along her cervix. I love to feel my wife's cervix while we are having sex.

"What else did you do with him?" I ask her.

Cassie begins to moan as my log saws along her swelling clitoris. "Everything. He loved my pussy though. Do you love my pussy, Owen? Say it. Say that you love my pussy, baby." She puts her hands on my shoulders as she leans back a little and just enjoys the way I feel inside her vagina.

"I love your pussy," I tell her while cupping her breasts in my hands. My fingers run swirls over each nipple as they get hard. "I loved seeing you with him, Cass. I loved the idea that he came inside you. That's why I got so hard last night. I was thinking about him squirting his jism into you." I'm getting close as my wife moves along my pole. It's been a long time since I've been so horny for her. Now that we're fucking and talking about what happened, my entire viewpoint has begun to change.

"I love your cock," Cassie says as she humps me a little faster. "Owen...*fuck...*" Her small body shakes as she gets closer and closer to having an orgasm. I can't wait to fill her little pussy with my thick man sauce.

"I wish I could have been there to watch you both together," I tell her. "I wish I could have smelled the sex in that room, Cass. Fuck, I would have joined in and helped him fuck you if I had been there." I laugh a little at the thought as our bodies move faster and faster. "I would love to watch him fuck you."

"Really?" Her eyes look deeply into mine as she begins to come. "Owen...*ahhhh...*" My wife throws her head back as she orgasms hard. *"Nahhh...ohhhh...ohhhhhh!!!"* Cassie is loud as her ass moves fast on my lap. This sudden increase in speed also begins to work on me as well.

*"OHHHH!!!"* I spurt hard into my wife's tight snapper as I hold on tightly to her breasts. *"FUCK!!! Uhhhh...shit...AHHHHH!!!"* My balls hurt as I push everything I have into my wife's pussy. *"Oh...uhhhh..."*

*"Owen...Owen..."* Cassie soon slows down and simply bends forward to rest her head on my shoulder. I can feel her pussy juices and my own semen slowly oozing over my balls and onto the patio chair. What started

out as a somewhat contentious conversation has turned into something much better.

"Cass," I begin as I kiss her neck lightly. "Oh, fuck, what just happened?"

She sits up and looks into my eyes. "We love each other, baby. You and I belong together, no matter what has happened." She pauses before asking, "Were you serious about Wyatt and me having sex while you watch?"

I swallow hard. "Yeah, I think I would like that. I want to see him fuck you and I might even want to help out a little."

"Oh, I love that plan." Cassie smiles as she leans back toward me. We kiss hard for a minute before she sits back up and lifts herself away from my limp pecker. She then kneels down again and takes my cock into her mouth.

"Geez, honey," I say as I grip the sides of my seat. She moves her mouth up and down it for a minute before pulling away from me. "I also cleaned him off like this when we were finished." Cassie allows a wicked grin as she looks at me. "I'll call him, okay? I'll see what he thinks about your idea. If that's okay, anyway."

I nod my head. "Yeah, I would like that," I reply.

"Then, I guess divorce is no longer on the table?" she asks.

"No, it's not." I smile at her. "I love you very much, Cassie. I'm sorry that I have been behaving like a complete asshole."

"You had good reason to be an asshole," she laughs. "I shouldn't have done what I did in public and I probably should have come to you with what I wanted to do with Wyatt. Maybe you would have agreed and maybe you wouldn't have, but still, at least it wouldn't have been behind your back.

I return the smile. "Ask him what he thinks of the idea. If he wants to do it, we could meet him somewhere." Cassie nods her head and gets up from between my legs. She retreats into the house and I'm left to look at my shrinking cock. "Damn, Owen," I say with a laugh as I think about how things have changed so quickly. "You really are a horny bastard, aren't you?" All this time my reaction has been more sexual than angry. There was frustration inside me because Cassie had fun with Wyatt and left me out of it. That will soon change if he agrees to meet us for sex. I can't wait to hear his answer to my wife's invitation.

# Chapter Eight: Breakfast and Conversation

"It's a nice little restaurant," Cassie tells me as we walk toward the front door of *Gaston's* in the city. We make our way inside and are greeted almost immediately by a young man at a podium.

"Do you have a reservation?"

"Yes. The Johnson table please." I look over at my wife as I hear the name. It's not our name, so it doesn't make sense as to why we would have a reservation under it.

"This way." We follow the young man as he leads us to the back of the restaurant. He opens a door and waves us in. There are only three tables in here, one of them occupied by a man with his back to us.

"We'll have whatever he's having," Cassie tells the young man. He nods his head and leaves the room. We make our way to the table where the other man is sitting. As he turns to look at us, I feel my heart skip a beat.

"Well, we finally get to meet." Wyatt Felton stands to his feet and offers his hand. At first, I'm not so sure whether I want to greet him or punch him in the mouth. I could possibly do both, first by shaking his hand and then smacking him. After all, he is the guy who has been having sex with Cassie. Though my mind reels with these thoughts, I keep my cool and shake his hand.

"You'll have to excuse Owen," she says to the other man. "He's still a little keyed up over what has been happening, but I think he's in a much better place now." She pats my back before we sit down at the table with the celebrity.

"It's pretty brazen to actually show up here in our own town," I tell him while shaking my head. "You're a ballsy guy, huh?"

Wyatt laughs. "You might say that. I think that I just don't like beating around the bush."

"Unless it's someone else's wife's bush." The remark from me is surprising to us all after I make it. "Look, I'm sorry. It's just that I didn't know that we were coming to see you. I've not had time to sort things out before we got here."

"No one knows," Cassie tells me. "We don't want the paparazzi to find us here."

"And it took one hell of a deception to get them away from my home in Beverly Hills," Wyatt tells us. "I had three lookalikes go in separate directions, one after the other. Then I hopped on a private jet that belongs to a friend who has business here anyway. So, when we landed it didn't draw any attention from the local media."

"That's good," my wife replies. "She looks over at me. "Are you still alright being here? You told me that you wanted me to call him."

I chuckle. "I thought you would call him and then tell me what he thought about our idea. I didn't know that I would actually be meeting him upfront."

"I wanted to get to know you a little before anything happens," Wyatt tells me. "Cassie has spoken really highly about you."

I raise an eyebrow. "You talked about me during your time together?"

"Of course I did," my wife replies. "It wasn't like I was trying to leave you, baby. We talked about both of our spouses."

"Ah, the wife," I say with a nod. "She's pretty pissed off at you."

Wyatt sighs. "She's been upset with me for the last year or so. This isn't a new thing with her. As a matter of fact, she's been seeing another man for the last several months. Our marriage was falling apart long before I met Cassie." He reaches over and takes my wife's hand, causing a flush of jealousy to fill me. Just because he has decided things are over with his wife doesn't mean that he can move into my marriage.

"We're happily married," I say as I look at their hands. Wyatt pulls away from my wife as he clears his throat.

"I mean nothing by it. All this is just a sign of affection for Cassie. I'm not after her to make her mine, Owen. All I ask is to be allowed to enjoy her company once in a while." I can see by the way that they look at each other that they really enjoy their time together.

"And Owen wants to be a part of that," Cassie says. "He asked me a few days ago to try to set it up. He wants to watch and maybe even join in with us."

Wyatt grins. "Have you had a threesome before, Owen?"

I shake my head. "No, I haven't. As a matter of fact I've only had sex with my wife since we've been together." It's meant as a cheap shot at the other man, though it doesn't appear immediately that he takes it as such.

"Well, it's lots of fun," he replies. "My wife and I had threesomes with a few others here and there when we first got married. Then she got weird about it. Almost possessive whenever I would have a scene with another woman on a television episode. That wasn't fun at all."

"And it's not much fun to get drawn into a public thing, either," I reply. "The two of you shouldn't have been out and about with each other. It has made life shitty for me."

"I'm sorry," my wife says for about the third time. "We were just being together. It shouldn't have happened the way it did. If I could change that, I would."

"And I told her that she shouldn't be out with me," Wyatt adds. "But your sweet wife..." He pauses and just looks at Cassie. Though he's not in love with her, he obviously enjoys the thought of being with her. "Anyway, that is a very unfortunate thing, Owen. I wish we could take it back."

"Me too." A server walks into the room with a bottle of wine and three glasses.

"Here you are, sir." She smiles widely at Wyatt. It's obvious that she knows who he is as her ability to contain herself barely holds.

"Thank you, miss. Look, if you can keep this a secret, I'll tip you really well. Alright?"

"Maybe a picture too?" she asks. "Please?"

Wyatt nods his head while smiling at the young woman. "I'll allow a picture too. Just don't tell anyone about it until tomorrow, okay? I don't want to be bothered by the reporters."

"No problem. I'll keep my mouth shut." The server turns and walks away, a huge smile on her face.

Cassie giggles. "I'm not so sure that she won't tell someone today or tonight, Wyatt."

"Well, I would chase her down and kill her, but I left my pistols at home." He laughs along with my wife and I simply smile. It's funny, but I don't feel like enjoying a laugh with the celebrity just yet.

"So, wine?" He picks up the bottle and shows it to us. Cassie nods and I do as well. Wyatt then pours some wine into each of the three glasses and picks his up. "To a nice time together."

"Yeah, that sounds great." I know I sound like someone trying to wet down whatever is going on here, but that's just who I am right now. Maybe that will change soon.

We each have a drink of wine before Cassie asks, "Owen, do you still want to see us together in bed?"

Shrugging my shoulders, I answer, "I guess I would. I mean, it would be better than hearing about it on the news or seeing a video online, right?"

Wyatt laughs. "That video was partially my fault, by the way. I think someone hacked my Apple account and got it from there."

"So, you made the video? On purpose?"

"I thought I told you that," Cassie answers before the other man can say anything. "Wyatt and I liked taking videos and pictures of ourselves."

"And the other pictures, like the one with you topless at the pool?"

"That wasn't us," Wyatt tells me. "The paparazzi got into that area without permission. The police were called, but we never knew which one snapped it." He grimaces after taking another sip of his wine. "They hound me all the damned time. Even when I go to see my own family, they're waiting on me in the bushes. I've tried to reason with them and even offer them something in return for them leaving me alone sometimes, but they're like damned ants crawling through a window. They're relentless."

I can understand his aggravation with people constantly trying to take pictures or videos of Wyatt. After all, I've had to live through some of that over the last week. However, he chose this life. I did not. This is probably part of what still bothers me even today. I have been made to suffer through this attention even though I didn't ask for it.

"So, you want to see us together?" Wyatt asks. "Will you be as jealous as you are now if we do that?"

"I don't know," I admit. "I might be. I'll try not to be."

"He needs to be included somehow," my wife tells him. "I don't think he will mind so much if Owen is a part of what's happening." She smiles at me.

"Good." The star leans toward me at the table. "It doesn't bother me to have a threesome with another guy in the room, but I think that you should know that I don't swing in another tree, if you get my meaning."

"Yeah, I think I do," I reply. "I don't either."

"Then we can enjoy your wife together, right? You'll be alright with that?" Wyatt smiles widely as he awaits my answer.

My cock stiffening, I tell him, "I'm okay to have a threesome with you both."

"And you won't go after me if I push my dick into Cassie, right? I can fuck her hard if I want to?"

"Oh, Wyatt," Cassie says while smiling and blushing. It's strange to see the difference in how she feels about him saying something so vulgar to how she feels about me saying practically the same thing.

"I can take it," I promise. "As long as we all understand that Cassie is my wife. I won't be letting her go. Sex is one thing, but you don't have permission to go after her heart."

"He hasn't," Cassie replies with a smile. She reaches over and takes my hand. "You're the only one for me, baby. What Wyatt and I have is purely physical."

"Very physical," he adds. "I have a hotel room nearby if you both are ready to go there."

"Already?" My eyes grow wide.

"Well, sure. Why wait until tomorrow or another day? We all three want this, right? Let's do it, then." Wyatt stands to his feet and offers his hand to my wife. She takes it and he helps her to her feet. I stand up from my seat as well. "I'll get the tab for the drinks. I don't think they'll mind since I've paid for this room already."

We make our way to the doorway of the room and then to the front entrance of the restaurant. There is an SUV waiting nearby where a driver holds the door open for three of us. We get inside and soon we are making our way to the hotel where Wyatt is staying. It seems that we will soon be having sex with each other. My first threesome is about to begin.

# Chapter Nine: Going for Glory

"It's a nice room, Wyatt," Cassie comments as we close the door behind us. "I didn't think the Hilton here had such a large suite."

"This was a nice surprise to me too," he admits. "Honestly, I thought that what I might get wouldn't be what I'm accustomed to, but it really is very well cared for." Wyatt motions toward a refrigerator nearby. "I have some refreshments inside there if you would like anything."

Cassie goes to the refrigerator and opens it up. After finding some wine coolers, she pulls three bottles out and hands them to us. We open them and enjoy sips of the cold, lightly alcoholic beverages.

"I love strawberry wine coolers," my wife says with a smile as she puts her bottle down on a table and walks over to Wyatt. Cassie wraps her arms around his neck and they begin to kiss deeply, their tongues moving in and out of each other's mouths. I say nothing as I simply stand and watch the two of them together. My cock begins to harden a little.

"You taste so much better than a wine cooler," he tells her. Wyatt begins to unbutton my wife's blouse, a blue number that she wore to the restaurant. As he does, she moves her hands around his blue jean's snap, opening it up quickly as his fingers nimbly move along the line of buttons between her breasts. I take a quick breath as Cassie pulls her blouse off after he finishes unbuttoning it.

"Wyatt," she moans as his hands push the cups of her bra up over each breast. He holds each one in his hands before leaning forward and pressing his lips against one of them. Cassie puts her hands on his head and runs her fingers through his thick, blond hair as he sucks on her nipple.

"Shit," I say quietly as I put my own wine cooler down and then unbutton my shirt. Though I'm not quite ready yet to get involved with them, I do want to be ready for whatever might happen. I'm hard already, pre-coming inside my pants as I pull off my clothes.

The male heartthrob then moves toward Cassie's shorts. He pulls them down to reveal a pair of thong panties. He strips these off as well before picking up my wife and tossing her to the bed. Her soft, puffy labia shimmer with her own wetness as Wyatt finishes taking his clothes off. He then goes down on her and begins to lap at my wife's sweet nectar.

"Oh, shit, Wyatt," she squeaks as he tastes her goodness. "Oh, fuck." Her small body wriggles around on the bed beneath him as she enjoys the feeling of his tongue on her pussy. I get completely hard as I finish pulling off my own clothes. I can see that the other man in the room is well endowed with his package waggling from side to side just in front of him.

"You taste heavenly," he growls at my wife as he reaches for her round orbs. Squeezing her tits, Wyatt smiles at her and goes back down to continue eating her out. I pre-come as I watch the way Cassie pulls her legs back and simply enjoys her lover's ability to bring her to the brink of an orgasm.

Wyatt puts two fingers into my wife's pussy and begins to move them in and out of her quickly as his tongue flicks across her swollen lady bit. Cassie's legs go back even further as she bites her lower lip. There's a true talent in his mouth as he pleases her on the bed. I stroke my cock as I think about how I can be a part of what's going on. I don't want to stop Wyatt doing what he's doing right now. Cassie is enjoying it too much.

"You're so tight," he tells her between licks. "Cassie, I want to fuck you."

"Fuck me," she says immediately. I watch as Wyatt stands up and easily pulls her petite body toward him. Cassie is a spinner and very light. Her lover can manipulate her however he likes as he pokes into her tight muffin.

His large cock, at least nine inches long, buries deep into Cassie's sweet twat. She bucks a little as he finds her cervix and begins to thrust in and out of her. My wife grips the covers of the bed tightly as he has his way with her.

"You fucking little whore," he groans as he slowly slides his cock along the inside of her vagina. "Oh, you little she-devil." I pre-come some more as I hear the dirty talk coming from the television star. I wonder if he's ever had real sex with any of the female leads in any of his shows? If so, they were probably just as much into it as Cassie is right now.

"You're deep," she tells him as he pushes her knees to her chest. Wyatt intends to get as deep inside my wife as he can. "Fuck, you're so deep. *Fuck.*" Her face turns red as she grimaces.

"Come here," He growls as he pulls her hard toward him again. Each thrust into my wife causes her to move a little bit away from him, so he has to work to pull her back to him as he fucks her. "You're so damned tight."

I get up and walk over to the two people on the bed. Cassie opens her eyes and sees me. She reaches out and I let her take my hardness into her hand. As she begins to pump my cock, pre-come oozes from my pisshole.

"Shit," I mutter as Cassie milks my pole. "This is so fucking hot." I can see very well Wyatt's meat as he moves in and out of my wife. Thinking about the way he has come inside her before makes me smile a little as I reach down and pull on one of her nipples.

"Owen, *ow.*" She frowns at me, but I pull on it again before moving around and pressing my cock to her lips. Cassie opens her mouth and lets me push my johnson in and across her tongue.

"There you go," I say to her breathlessly. "Suck it, babe." Cassie knows how to suck a dick, and that's one thing that has kept our marriage a little spicier over the years. Any time I've wanted a blow job, she's given it to me. Even now, she seems eager to please me as she gets another man's penis inside her vagina.

"Fuck, Cassie," Wyatt moans. "You hot little slut."

"A fucking slut," I agree as I push my cock into her throat. She gags a little, but keeps sucking on me as I slowly thrust in and out across her tongue.

"Here. Let's change." Wyatt pulls out of Cassie and I back out of her mouth. He helps her to get on all-fours and then enters her from behind. He slaps her ass hard, causing her to grimace before I push my cock back into her mouth. Almost as if we have put her on a spit to roast, we are poking Cassie from both ends.

"Oh, this is it," I say as I put my fingers in my wife's hair and pull her to me. The sensation of mouth fucking her like this is intense and I smile as she gags a little on the head of my manhood. "Swallow my pre-come," I tell her. Cassie does swallow occasionally to keep the liquid lubricant from escaping her lips. Her small body quakes with excitement as Wyatt rakes the head of his own cock along her G-spot.

*"Mmmmm..."* Cassie can't say much with my shaft in her mouth, but Wyatt and I seem to both understand that she's getting close to an orgasm.

"I'm going to come soon," he admits as his balls slap her labia. "Fuck, I don't think I can hold out for very long." There is a sort of tug-o-war going on between us as we screw each end of my wife. I wonder if she feels just as good as we do as we have sex altogether.

I hear a sound. I look over and see the doorknob on the hotel room door turning. The door is locked, though. Magnetically. There's no way anyone could possibly open it. I'm wrong, though. There is someone on the other side who has found a way to gain entry to this room. A woman, possibly in her thirties and wearing a hotel maid's garb, walks in with a large camera. She begins snapping pictures of us as we fuck each other.

"I'm sorry," the woman says as she takes pictures and possibly some video footage. I want to pull out of Cassie's mouth and push the woman out of the room through the door, but I don't. I'm too close to coming. I think the other two people with me are also too close to coming to care that someone is watching.

"Oh, holy fuck...*UHHHH!!!"* Wyatt begins to come hard, his man gravy spurting into my wife's womb and even dribbling out around his cock as he slams into her over and over again. *"Oh, baby. Cassie...FUCK!!!"* He pulls hard on her hips as I try to keep my own manhood buried inside her mouth. However, my wife bites down a little as she begins to come. I worry at first that she might bite off my prized possession.

*"Mmmmmm!!! MMMMMM!!!"* I thrust my cock to the back of her throat as she comes. *"Uttt...uttt...ACK!!!"* Cassie's throat opens up a little wider and I'm able to wedge my cock deep inside as I begin to spew out my jism.

I look over at the woman in the maid's outfit as she takes pictures of me coming into my wife's mouth. *"Motherfucker! MOTHERFUCKER!!! FUCK...oh, fuck...FUCK!!!"* I don't recall ever coming this hard with Cassie or any other woman before. *"OOHHHH!!! OOOOHHHHHH!!!"*

*"UTTT..."*

"You're choking her," the woman with the camera says. "Is this your fetish? Wyatt, is this the woman you've left your wife for? And her *husband?"* She keeps taking pictures as we each pull our soaked dicks out of my wife.

"Get out," I hear Wyatt say as he walks toward the woman. She takes a few more pictures of his dick as well as mine and then she flees the room.

"Fuck," Cassie says as she collapses to the bed and takes a deep breath. "Who was that?"

"Paparazzi," Wyatt replies. "I'll bet that girl at the restaurant didn't keep her mouth shut." He frowns while shaking his head and looking at my wife. "Are you alright? We didn't hurt you, did we?"

Cassie laughs. "Well, you both really shoved your dicks into me hard. I liked it, though."

"Me too," I say as I sit back on the bed with my wet phallus between my legs. "Dammit, that was intense. I didn't think that I could really do that with you."

Wyatt smiles. "It gets easier once you give into it the first time. I've had enough practice over the years."

Cassie shakes her head and smirks. "You mean to say that I'm not your first true lover?"

He laughs as he sits down on the bed beside her. "No, but you've got to be the best one yet. Even better than my soon to be ex-wife."

"I had better be that good." Cassie looks over at me. "So, are you glad that you did this with me, baby? Did you enjoy it?"

I chuckle as I look from her to Wyatt and then back again. "I don't know that I like the fact that there are pictures and maybe videos of what we just did, but then again there were already journalists after us all. You know, I did like it. It was fun. You let me throat fuck you really well, too."

"You're so vulgar," Cassie says as she shakes her head and laughs.

"Hey, sex is vulgar," I tell her with a smile. "Don't hate me for just saying it like it is. You're great."

"And so are you." My wife seems very happy as she rests on the bed beside Wyatt Felton, his spunk slowly creeping out of her wet pussy. My cock hardens a little as I consider going to her and fucking her the same way and in the same place as the other man. Sure, it would mean sloppy seconds, but I really don't care. Sex with Cassie is great regardless of what is inside her sweet pussy.

# Chapter Ten: Work and Personal Life

I make my way into the regional vice president's office and have a seat just across from him at his desk. "Thank you for coming in this morning," Ray says with a large smile on his face. "I'm glad that you've come back as a new man, Owen."

Nodding, I reply, "I feel like a new man now. The time off seems to have helped me put things into perspective." I watch as he opens up his laptop and looks at the screen in front of him.

"I can see here that the two problem managers we had are no longer managers at the two stores?" Ray looks up at me. He's obviously pleased that I've taken care of what had become a thorn in the company's side.

"Yeah, I let them go and replaced them with two assistant managers who seemed ready for the challenge," I tell him.

"Even your friend?"

"Even Aaron," I reply. "Look, I thought about what you said about not letting that friendship get in the way of what had to be done, and I think I was doing that for a while. I gave Aaron plenty of chances to improve, and he kept screwing things up. Even his assistant managers were threatening to quit if I didn't get rid of him soon. So, Aaron is gone now."

"And better ones are in place, I see." Ray turns his eyes back to his laptop screen. "Our profits at those two locations are already up. Things seem to be turning around, thanks to your decisive actions."

"Yes, sir, I believe that things will be much better for those stores." I smile at my boss, glad that he once again sees me as a capable regional manager. However, I become concerned as he decides to ask me a question.

"You wouldn't allow your personal life to become a hindrance to your work, would you, Owen?"

I shake my head. "Of course not. I've always kept the two separate."

"I see." He looks back at his laptop screen. He slowly turns it to face me so that I can see what is there. "This seems pretty interesting." It's a photograph of me, Cassie, and Wyatt Felton in the hotel room from a couple of weeks ago. The pictures the fake hotel maid took have apparently started to get out online.

"Um, I don't know what to say to that."

Ray grins slightly. "Look, I've told you the story about my ex-wife, right? So, I've seen some really crazy stuff in my life. I just want to know that this sort of thing doesn't become the sort of thing that the board of directors will need to know about. This could be just a little embarrassing to us, after all."

"Yeah, I can see that," I say before adding, "But this seems to be photoshopped. I mean, I hate that guy. There's no way that I would have sex with my wife with another man that I hate as much as him."

"It looks pretty convincing, though," Ray says as he turns the laptop back to himself. "It says here that it's real. If board members saw this, they would likely think the same thing."

"That's a gossip magazine site. They're not really known for great reporting, Ray. Honestly, someone thought that they could make money on some kind of a cheap photoshop job." This is the story that my wife and I decided that we would tell people when the images finally came out. Wyatt agreed to say the same thing so that my wife and I could at least save some of our personal life from the constant threat of the paparazzi.

"Okay. I'll buy that. For now." Ray smiles. "Just be sure that whatever your extracurricular activities are, you keep them between you and your wife...or whomever they involve."

"I'll be sure to do that," I say while nodding my head. "Anything else, sir?"

"Nah. Hell of a job you're doing, Owen. Keep it up." I stand up from my seat and shake Ray's hand before turning and leaving his office. I'm not sure whether a crisis has been averted or that he simply wanted to know if that was a real picture of the three of us together.

As I get on the elevator, my phone buzzes inside my pocket. I'm surprised to be able to get a call inside here, but I take it. "Hello?"

"It's your darling wife," Cassie says to me. "How is your day going so far?"

"Pretty good," I tell her. "And yours?"

"It's okay. I miss you."

"Miss me? Aren't you going from doctor to doctor to sell those new drugs your company is hocking? You should be too busy to miss me."

Cassie laughs. "I'm waiting to see a doctor right now. Her waiting room is full of patients, so they'll probably make me wait for a while. You know how irritating it can be to see a pharmaceutical rep go in to see a doctor while you're waiting to get some kind of treatment."

"Yeah, that's happened several times to me," I reply. "Some patients might be willing to revolt if they have to wait too long." Moving the conversation along, I tell her, "I have just left Ray's office. He's seen some of the pictures from our time in the hotel room. That maid has been passing them to websites.

"Shit," she says quietly. "What did he say about them?"

"It's fine," I tell her. "I explained that they're just photoshopped images that someone's made a little money off of. Hopefully that will keep his imagination at bay for now."

"And if it doesn't?"

"Well, then, he might fire me." I laugh a little, but my wife doesn't seem to find the thought so amusing. "Look, Ray just told me to be sure to keep my private life private and away from the public eye. He doesn't want me to embarrass the board over something like that."

"Yeah. Wyatt wants to see us again."

I frown. "I don't think that's a great idea, Cass." The elevator doors open and I get out. After getting to my office, I close the door and sit down at my desk.

"He's really into what we did, Owen. He wants to see us together again if it's possible."

"I know, but he's too popular, baby. He has paparazzi all over him, Cass. If we do that again, we'll probably get caught and that might trigger

Ray to do something about me. He likes me, but he won't have any other option than to terminate me from the job if the board begins to groan about it. I don't want to get fired over having sex with Wyatt Fucking Felton."

"Why do you still call him that? He's been nice to you, right?" Cassie sighs. She really does like to have sex with Wyatt, and I can understand why. However, we have to be smart about what we do from now on if we want to have a threesome without the paparazzi taking pictures of us. An actor or celebrity is just too high profile to meet up with as far as the paparazzi are concerned.

"Then, we need to find someone else? Someone not as popular or well known?"

"That would be fun, don't you think?" I reply. "There are plenty of other guys out there who could really eat you out just like Wyatt can, my love. We should at least give it a try. What do you say?"

My wife doesn't answer for a few seconds. Then she says, "Okay. Let's do that, then. I'll tell Wyatt that we're going to wait for things to cool down before we meet him again."

"Good idea," I reply. "We won't upset him right now. Maybe we could get back together with him when the time is right."

"So, who should it be, then?" Cassie asks as she chuckles.

"Maybe your cousin, Tracy? I think she could have a lot of fun with us."

Cassie laughs. "Uh, no. That's gross. She's a woman and she's my cousin. No way, Owen."

"Well, it's my turn to be the one in the middle, right?"

My wife laughs again. "I guess we could each wear strap-on cocks, huh? She could shove hers into your ass and I could gag you with mine."

"Wait. That's not what I mean, Cass." We both laugh as we consider what to do for the next time. My wife knows that I like to joke around, but she also knows that I'm at least somewhat serious about the request. No, of course it wouldn't be her cousin, but that's beside the point. There are women out there who would love to have a threesome with us. All we have to do is look for one that my lovely wife would be happy to let me play with. It would be a great time for the both of us, but especially for me.

"I'll think about the other woman thing if you agree that it might be another man instead."

I sigh. "Sure. I'll go along with that."

"Great." Cassie giggles. "Well, I'll let you go now. They've just called me back to see the doctor. I love you, Owen. I'll see you later."

I smile. "I love you too, sexy girl." She hangs up and I put my phone down on top of my desk. Thinking about all that we did with Wyatt, I wonder if Cassie and I could really connect on the same level with another person in the same way we did with him. Will we both be attracted to the thought of having someone else in bed with us? Judging from our most recent experience, I think we would have a great time no matter who it happens to be with. As long as I don't have to worry about her getting into some other celebrity's bed behind my back, I'll be fine with whomever we end up having sex with. As long as Cassie is with me and we're both enjoying ourselves, everything will be just fine. Our life will be very interesting from here on out. Hopefully not so interesting that the paparazzi will take an interest.

THE END

# Don't miss out!

Visit the website below and you can sign up to receive emails whenever Karly Violet publishes a new book. There's no charge and no obligation.

https://books2read.com/r/B-A-GIXE-JDTQB

BOOKS 2 READ

Connecting independent readers to independent writers.

Did you love *Hotwife Hotel Cheating Exposed - A Wife Watching Hot Wife Romance Novel*? Then you should read *Hotwife Exchange For Debt Payments - A Hotwife Wife Sharing Wife Watching Romance Novel*[1] by Karly Violet!

[2]

***Would you willingly allow another man to take your wife to repay a debt of $100k?***

This was precisely the situation that Layden found himself in.

When out of thin air, he found $100k had suddenly appeared in the joint account he shared with his wife, Terri

The naive husband was confident the money belonged to him and pursued speculative investments that were doomed to fail

And when they did indeed fail, it transpired the money was transferred to him erroneously from unscrupulous characters.

---

1. https://books2read.com/u/me9opr

2. https://books2read.com/u/me9opr

And when it became clear, there was no way to repay the sudden debt they were demanding ........

**........Layden has no choice but to consider loaning his wife's body as payment for debt!**

*This scorching hot 20,000 word novel features a naive husband suddenly finding himself in debt to a dangerous man with no option other than to loan his wife's body for repayment.*

Read more at https://www.patreon.com/karlyviolet.

# About the Author

Sign up to my mailing list to receive the two free epilogues for 'A Hotwife Adventure' and 'Hotwife Training' and to stay up to date on all of my latest releases! http://eepurl.com/c3ICWf Sign up to my Patreon account and receive exclusive Hotwife stories every month and sexy scenes every week! https://www.patreon.com/karlyviolet

Read more at https://www.patreon.com/karlyviolet.

# About the Publisher

www.ingramcontent.com/pod-product-compliance
Ingram Content Group UK Ltd.
Pitfield, Milton Keynes, MK11 3LW, UK
UKHW041822200726
13854UKWH00001BA/438